THE CHAMPAK STORY BOX

RUPA

Published by
Rupa Publications India Pvt. Ltd 2022
7/16, Ansari Road, Daryaganj
New Delhi 110002

Sales Centres:
Allahabad Bengaluru Chennai
Hyderabad Jaipur Kathmandu
Kolkata Mumbai

This is a work of fiction. Names, characters, places and incidents are either the product of the author's imagination or are used fictitiously and any resemblance to any actual person, living or dead, events or locales is entirely coincidental.

ISBN: 978-93-5520-380-9

First impression 2022

10 9 8 7 6 5 4 3 2 1

Printed in India

TABLE OF CONTENTS

THE KING OF MISERS....5
AN ADVENTURE OF A LIFETIME....11
THE GRASS IS GREENER....16
TREASURE EARNED....21
FOOD OR FRIENDS....27
A GLOW IN THE DARK....33
PANGY, THE SHY PANGOLIN....38
EMAIL FROM SANTA CLAUS....46
FRUITS OF LABOUR....53
THE FLYING ELEPHANT....58
BHIM AND THE BOOK THIEF....65
JORAM....71
THE NAUGHTY DUCKLING....75
THE NEW NEIGHBOUR....81
MICE IN A CAGE....87

A TALE OF TWO FRIENDS 91

BRINGING THE HOUSE DOWN 96

THE TEN-GRAM WEAKLING 102

THE MANTIS PROBLEM 108

A FRIGHTENING GHOST 115

I CAN 122

A 'GHOST' STORY 128

LOOK BEFORE YOU LEAP 136

FORGETFUL PARI 140

THE KING OF MISERS

By Ramakant 'Kant'

Jojo the Jackal lived in Nandanvan. He was very **stingy** and whenever he went to the market he only bought the cheapest things even if they were of poor quality. He always tried to save money even though he had problems later on.

Once during summer, Jojo had to go to another city for work. Though it would take him two days to reach, he decided to

travel by train because it was the cheapest form of transport. As luck would have it, Jojo got a window seat, even though the train was packed.

Being the miser that he was, Jojo wanted to be the only one to feel the air coming from the window. He spread himself in such a manner that no one could get the cool air, except him.

With the window blocked, the other passengers started feeling stuffy and said, "Jojo, please sit properly so that we also can get some breeze..."

He glared at them and refused to move. Everyone soon realised that it was useless to talk to him.

HUNGER CALLS

The train CHUGGED along and soon it was lunch time. Many animals got down from the train to get food, and the delicious aroma made Jojo hungry. But he thought, "If I get down, then someone will steal my seat and take away my free cool breeze!"

A few sellers came up to his window but he found them too expensive and chose to stay hungry rather than spend the extra money they asked for. Several stations passed when finally he spotted a watermelon seller. He called him and thought, "Yes, I'll buy a watermelon. It is cooling, cheap and filling." He asked the watermelon seller for its price. "One watermelon is for ₹60," replied the seller.

Jojo found the watermelon very EXPENSIVE and argued with the seller to bring down its price. After bargaining for a long time, the seller agreed to sell it to Jojo for ₹40. Jojo gave him two ₹20 notes. Just as the seller handed him the watermelon, the train started.

SENSELESS AND STINGY!

Now, Jojo had a new problem. The windows had iron bars across them. Jojo was holding the watermelon in his hand but he could not bring it inside through the bars. By this time, the train had caught speed. Because he had been fighting with everyone in the compartment, they all refused to help him.

The next station was in an hour and Jojo held on to the watermelon. After all, how could he lose ₹40?

The train moved fast through the jungle. Branches and thorns hit Jojo's hands and even though they were covered in blood Jojo held the watermelon.

Finally taking pity on him, some animals advised that he pull the chain to stop the train. Others said he should throw the watermelon. But Jojo, who would not let go of a ₹40 watermelon, pay a penalty of ₹100 for pulling the chain? No way!

AT LAST!

An hour later, the train stopped. But it was still not possible to bring the watermelon inside without someone holding it for Jojo from the outside. Jojo, who still did not want to give up his window seat could not ask anyone in the compartment for help.

The animals outside were too BUSY boarding the train to care. He kept calling but no one bothered to hear him.

Jojo looked left and right when at last a monkey agreed to help. "Hi, I'm Monty. I can hold the watermelon for you," he said. "Then I'll come inside from the front door and give it to you," said Monty.

Jojo eyed him with suspicion but then handed him the watermelon. Jojo waited for Monty to come inside through the front door, but when he could not see Monty, he decided to get down from the train. This took a while because of the huge Crowd. However, by the time he got down, Monty disappeared with the watermelon.

THE CHASE

Jojo looked up and down the platform. He finally saw Monty with the watermelon near the exit. It was impossible to run fast in the crowd, yet Jojo chased after Monty.

In the course of the chase, he nearly landed on the tracks. At last, Jojo caught Monty. Snatching the watermelon from Monty he ran back to catch the train. This time he collided with the coolie's cart and fell. Even though he fell, he held onto the watermelon tightly!

Finally, the railway police picked him, "Take me to a government hospital, not a private one," said Jojo because he did not want to spend too much money. The doctors examined him and said that the **bone** of his left hand was broken. And even while the doctors were bandaging his arm, he held the watermelon firmly.

The police informed his family about the accident and his brother came to pick him up. While going home, Jojo did not forget to take the watermelon with him. He showed the watermelon to all those he met in Nandanvan and told them the whole story! On hearing about his adventure, everyone laughed heartily and called him the 'King of Misers'!

AN ADVENTURE OF A LIFETIME

By Kumud Kumar

Momo the Mouse lived with his family in the storeroom of a big hotel. They led a very comfortable life and Momo never complained. The only problem was that he was very adventurous and sometimes got into trouble.

MOMO EXPLORES THE HOTEL

As he grew older, so did his thirst for adventure. He slowly started to leave the storeroom and began exploring the rooms next to it. He began jumping on the soft beds and SPRINGY sofas. He would swing on the curtains and would even swim in the FOUNTAIN.

He would sneak into all the PARTIES at the hotel. He would nibble on the FOOD till he had a full stomach. There was no type of food that he hadn't tasted and loved. He danced to the beats of the music, and went home every night feeling happy.

Momo's family on the other hand would always shy away from such things. He began to enjoy this lifestyle so much that he decided to move out of the tiny storeroom and into a bigger place. He moved into the hotel's lawn.

Going to parties was much easier now and so was the view he had from his burrow.

THE HUNT

One day, as he was wandering in the lawns, enjoying the **SUNLIGHT**, the hotel's gardener spotted him. He **CHASED** him but Momo gave him the slip and dove into his burrow. But the gardener was not one to give up.

The garderner got a pipe and filled Momo's burrow with water. But mice live in burrows with many entry and exit points. When Momo noticed that his burrow was filling up with water, he stepped out of the exit on the other side of the compound wall.

OUTSIDE THE HOTEL WALLS

After he stepped out, Momo realised that he had jumped out of the frying pan and into the fire. He came face to face

with a cat. While he was an expert at giving any cat the slip inside the hotel, he had no idea about the world outside the hotel's walls.

He ran as fast as he could until he heard the sound of DOGS barking. Hearing the dogs, the cat gave up the chase. Momo climbed up a pipe and jumped back into the hotel's compound. He saw his burrow was wet so, he crawled into a pipe and fell asleep.

He felt so comfortable in the pipe that he overslept. When the gardener opened the pipe to water the plants the next morning, Momo was shot out of the pipe. He woke up with a start and quickly RAN away to safety.

BACK TO SQUARE ONE

The gardener once again followed Momo who ran inside the hotel's open-air café. A family was enjoying their breakfast

there and when they saw Momo, they screamed in fright calling out for help. The hotel staff rushed to them thinking they were in serious trouble.

When they found that there was a mouse in their hotel, they joined the gardener and ran after Momo. When Momo entered the gallery that had tiles, his feet began to slip. The gardener and the hotel staff were gaining on him. He thought he was gone for sure until the gardener lost his balance, slipped and FELL, tripping all the other staff members.

This gave Momo time to think. He realised that he was not far from the storeroom and quickly ran towards it.

Seeing the hotel staff SpRaWlEd on the floor, the guests laughed. The staff took it in sport and walked away laughing and got back to work. Momo went home to his family. He had had enough adventure for this lifetime and spent the rest of his days enjoying his life in a simple cosy storeroom.

THE GRASS IS GREENER

By Vivek Chakravarty

Dino the Donkey and Rinku the Rat worked at Ellie the Elephant's shop. Rinku **packed** the items for the customers while Dino handled their **bills** and accounts. Neither Dino nor Rinku were happy with their jobs.

NEW IDEAS

One morning, Dino and Rinku went to Ellie's HOUSE to discuss their problems.

"Sir, I'm tired of packing the goods and handing them over to the customers. From now on, I want to take the RESPONSIBILITY of handling the accounts," said Rinku.

"So, you are tired now? Handle the accounts for one day, and you'll realise how much attention and care it requires. Sir, I too want to exchange my duties," said Dino, angrily.

"Look, it's better if you keep doing what you have been doing for such a long time. You'll find it hard to adapt to new responsibilities. The grass is always GREENER on the other side," explained Ellie.

"Sir, please swap our roles," Dino insisted.

Ellie finally agreed. "All right, if that's what you want! From now onwards, Dino will pack the goods for the customers and Rinku will handle the accounts. Here's the key. Go and open the shop. I'll come soon."

"Thank you, Sir!"

THE SWAP

At the shop, Dino started PACKING the goods for the customers and Rinku started HANDLING the accounts.

Soon, Matty the Monkey came to the shop. "Where's Rinku? He's the one who usually packs our goods!" he asked, surprised.

"Do you want your goods or do you want to chitchat with Rinku? Tell me what you want and I'll pack it for you at once," said Dino, proudly.

"I want a bathing soap for monkeys, the one that softens the skin," said Matty.

"Here you go!" said Dino and handed a bar of SOAP to him.

"What's this? I asked for a bar of bath soap. This is a detergent soap. Do you want to ruin my skin?" asked Matty, IRRITABLY.

"I'm sorry, that was a mistake," said Dino and quickly FETCHED another soap.

"What's this, now? This is a TOILET soap. It seems you really want to damage my skin! I wonder where Rinku is. He would never make a mistake like this," said Matty and left the shop angrily.

"*Argh!* He has no patience! If only he waited a little longer, I'd have given him the soap he wanted!" thought Dino.

Ellie was furious to see a customer leave the shop without buying anything. But since Dino had been working for him for a long time, he did not say anything.

Soon, other customers came into the shop and Dino got busy attending to them.

Dino did not know where each item was stored in the shop, nor did he have any idea about which items were available and which were not. He was taking too long to help each customer with their orders.

Most customers got irritated and started complaining. Dino too got DISTRESSED because of this.

Meanwhile, since Rinku was poor in **mathematics**, he was barely managing the calculations for each order. And now with the **commotion** inside, he too started making mistakes.

By late evening, both Dino and Rinku were frustrated with their new jobs and realised that their old jobs were better.

They both now wanted their original duties. At night, after closing the **SHOP**, Dino and Rinku met outside.

A LESSON LEARNT

"Why don't we swap our jobs again?" they both said together.

"Our previous jobs were best suited for us," said Dino, and Rinku nodded. The next morning, when Ellie the Elephant entered the shop, he smiled. He was happy to see Dino and Rinku doing their old jobs again.

"Didn't I tell you that the grass is always greener on the other side? You both thought that the other's job was easier, but that's not the case!" said Ellie.

Dino and Rinku laughed and nodded.

TREASURE EARNED

By Manoj Roy

Justin the Bull was extremely **LAZY**. He spent his time doing nothing. He dreamt of becoming rich overnight without working for it. His friends tried to make him understand that he should do something worthwhile, but he refused to change his lazy behaviour.

TICKET TO A TREASURE

One morning as he stepped out of his house, he found a small red piece of paper outside his door.

"What is this?" he wondered as he picked it up.

"Wow! This seems like a ticket to some TREASURE," he said.

He went inside the house and started reading what was written on the paper.

It said, "Anyone who levels the road to the mountain shall get this treasure. A treasure that never ends!"

Justin was excited reading about the treasure but the condition to get to it was difficult.

"That road is extremely uneven and levelling it is a huge task. If I try to do it alone, it will take a lot of time. I think I should ask someone to help me," he thought.

He instantly thought of Bobby the Bear.

"Bobby would be perfect! He needs money urgently and is also free throughout the day. Let me talk to him."

"Are you absolutely sure that a treasure is hidden there?" asked Bobby as Justin informed him about the plan.

The question surprised Justin, but he was sure and said, "Even if there is no hidden treasure, we have nothing to lose. It will take us a maximum of one week to level the road. If we find the treasure, then great, otherwise we will just forget about it."

Bobby agreed as he found Justin's explanation logical.

THE SEARCH BEGINS

Both immediately took their tools and reached the place mentioned in the paper. They worked tirelessly from MORNING till evening.

At first, the task seemed difficult as they were not used to working this hard.

But soon they started liking the work and left in the morning after breakfast and would come back home late in the evening.

Slowly, their hard work paid off. The uneven rocky terrain now became a levelled road leading to the mountain.

"We have finished our job but we didn't find any treasure," cried Bobby.

Justin had no answer to this question. "You are right! We have finished the work as per the instructions on the paper but where is the treasure?"

THE REWARD

"Your treasure is here!" said a voice behind them.

They saw Robo the Rabbit standing there.

"Robo, is that you? What are you doing here?" asked Justin.

"I have come here to give you your reward. You both have worked so hard and deserve the treasure," said Robo, smiling widely.

The two of them did not understand what was happening.

"We needed two strong animals to construct this road. I had observed that both of you were idle at home for a long time. I knew that you would never agree to work on the road if I asked you, hence, I had to make up the story about the treasure," explained Robo.

"Does that mean there is no treasure here?" asked Bobby sadly.

"Please don't be upset! You will soon get your treasure," said Robo and patted Bobby's shoulders.

"Take this," he said and handed them a box.

"Now what is this?" asked Justin irritably.

"It has ₹30,000 in it. This is the amount that was to be paid

for this work. You can divide it amongst yourselves and if you are ready, I have another treasure that I have to discuss with you. That one is worth ₹50,000. So, will I see you both again in two days for the second one?" asked Robo.

Justin and Bobby looked at each other.

"Not in two days, we will see you in one day," said Bobby promptly.

"In one day? Why?" Robo asked with SURPRISE.

"It is because we are worried that if we get back to our old habits long enough, we will become lazy again," said Justin.

The three of them LAUGHED.

TREASURE FIND

PUZZLE TIME

Bobby the Bear and Justin the Bull are at Treasure Island to collect treasure. They reached here at 6 AM. Read the hints and calculate what time they will reach the other three ports to collect more treasure.

* Answer on the last page

FOOD OR FRIENDS

By Parul Maheshwari

As soon as Myra the Squirrel's summer VACATION began, her appetite grew by leaps and bounds. If one day she ate a BISCUIT CAKE, on another, she would crave pizzas and BURGERS. And while she was having a good time, her mother was tired of taking care of her HUGE appetite.

MYRA LEARNS TO COOK

One day, Myra's mother said, "Myra, you're getting older. Why don't you help me out around the house? ”

Myra was not too keen on the idea at first, but one day she saw her mother baking her favourite cake and decided to watch her. After a while, as she started spending more time in the **kitchen**, her mother taught her simple things. Her mother taught her how to **wash** the vegetables and STORE them in the **FRIDGE**. She taught her the names of various **INGREDIENTS** too. Once she had learned this, she taught her how to prepare simple things like rice, dal and other dishes. Myra had a lot of fun and loved helping her mother.

When Chhaya the Mouse's mother heard that Myra had been learning how to **cook**, she asked Chhaya to learn too. Chhaya refused and told her that she was not interested in cooking and just wanted to enjoy her summer vacation.

Ellie the Elephant, Fifi the Fox and Jojo the Jackal also just wanted to spend their summer vacation not doing anything. When Myra told them that they should try to learn something new during their holidays like **painting**, **SWIMMING** or **music**, they refused to listen. They made fun of her and laughed but Myra didn't feel bad.

A COOKING CONTEST

One day, Myra and all her friends were at the park when they noticed a **poster** on the **BULLETIN BOARD**.

It was an announcement about a cooking contest in the colony.

The contest was called 'Kitchen Animals' and would take place in one week. The child who prepared the best dish would be awarded a bicycle. The chance of winning a bicycle interested them all. Chhaya, Ellie, Fifi and Jojo didn't know how to cook; they decided to spend the next seven days at home learning how to.

THE EFFECTS OF THE COMPETITION

Now, Myra was sad, despite it being their summer holidays, she could no longer meet her friends. When she offered to teach them how to cook, her friends weren't interested. They felt insecure about the fact that Myra was already a good cook and her chances of winning were much higher than theirs. So, they told her that they didn't need her help.

The day of the cooking contest was drawing near. Myra was feeling very lonely. It had been so long since she had seen any of her FRIENDS. While they were worried about the competition, Myra was not. She wasn't even interested in winning the cycle. The only reason she wanted to participate in the COMPETITION was that she would finally be able to meet her friends.

When Myra asked her mother what she should prepare for

the competition, her mother suggested that she should cook anything her heart desired.

"After all," she added. "This competition is being conducted so that children can learn something new and have fun. So you should decide what you would like to make and I'll help you with your practice batches."

Meanwhile, Chhaya, Ellie, Fifi and Jojo were also trying to learn how to make one dish each so that they could present it for the competition and win the cycle.

THE COMPETITION

On the day of the competition, all the children assembled at

the **venue**. To win the cycle, they would need to complete two rounds and move on to the third where they would have to prepare their special dish.

The first round involved identifying EXOTIC vegetables by sight. Myra and all her friends, except Fifi and Jojo, couldn't.

In the second round, all the children were given a bowl of ice-cream and asked to name all the INGREDIENTS in it. Ellie, who had barely cleared the previous round, was getting really nervous because he was not able to identify half the flavours. Not only was Ellie **ELIMINATED** in this round, Chhaya was too.

THE REAL WINNER

In the final round, it was Myra against three other participants from the colony. Myra prepared pudding and won the competition.

Chhaya, Ellie, Fifi and Jojo regretted the fact that they didn't learn how to cook sooner. They were also ashamed of the way they treated Myra and refused her offer of teaching them how to cook. If they had, they would have had a better chance at winning the **bicycle**.

When Myra was handed the **keys**, she ran towards her friends. "This is not my bike," she said. "This is our bike."

That's when Chhaya, Ellie, Fifi and Jojo realised how much love Myra had for them, they all gave her a big hug. They congratulated her on her **victory** and shouted, "Hip-hip. Hurray! Hip-hip Hurray for Myra!"

~ ☼ ~

A GLOW IN THE DARK

By Ramakant 'Kant'

Staying awake all night is unhealthy. But some animals and birds stay awake in the night and sleep in the day. These animals are called 'nocturnal'.

Nandavan too had **nocturnal** animals, Ruby the Owl was one of them and so were Bubbly the Bat, Henry the Hedgehog, Hillary the Hyena and Rikky the Rat. They played, ate and talked in the night.

A STRANGE CREATURE APPEARS

One summer night, Ruby, Henry, Hillary, Bubbly and

Rikky were talking and enjoying the cool breeze, when suddenly they saw a spark of light which had come out of nowhere!

Everyone was alarmed. Though they knew what moonlight looked like, this was different. It was like a SHINING dot which was moving. All of them were alert, lest it would harm them.

Then they heard someone speak. The voice said, "Friends! Do not get alarmed! I am Frisky the Firefly. I have a special light-producing organ under my stomach so I shine at night."

Saying this, Frisky sat on a plant nearby.

GETTING TO KNOW FRISKY

All the friends were impressed. Ruby said, "We have not seen a firefly before. You are beautiful and you glow brightly! Are you visiting us or have come to stay in Nandavan?"

"I would like to stay here in this JUNGLE with you all, if you do not mind," replied Frisky.

Ruby said, "You are welcome to stay in Nandavan!"

Henry asked, "How come you decided to move to Nandavan?"

Frisky was in tears as she said, "I was flying with my family when we got separated. While trying to find my way back home, I reached here."

Hillary said, "Welcome to Nandavan, Frisky! We do not know much about you, but you appear to be nice. I am sure we all will enjoy your **company**."

"Frisky, you are our friend now. We will play together and have fun," said Ricky and hugged her.

ORGANISING A TALENT SHOW

Ruby, Henry, Hillary, Bubbly and Rikky decided that they should organise a **talent** show and Frisky's glow **dance** would be the highlight of the event.

It was decided that the show would be held on a new-moon day as there would be no moonlight and Frisky's light could be seen at its best.

As darkness fell, all animals gathered under a big **BANYAN** tree, which was the usual place for such events.

Bubbly, Hillary, Henry and Rikky all performed. When it was pitch dark, Ruby stood on the stage and presented Frisky to the jungle audience.

"Dear friends! I'd like to introduce Frisky the Firefly who has just moved to Nandavan. Her mere presence will speak about her beauty," announced Ruby.

Frisky came on the stage and danced. She was a tiny insect, but her dance was visible to everyone and it looked as if a star had come down from the sky. When it was over, everyone CLAPPED. Frisky was very happy.

A PLACE TO CALL HOME

After the show, King Sher Khan said, "Frisky! It is nice to have you here. You dance very well, and you have your own spark. We appreciate your UNIQUENESS. We are glad that you have decided to make this jungle your home."

All animals clapped and CELEBRATED Frisky, the new star and their new friend!

Everyone helped Frisky look for her family, and soon they too moved to Nandavan because of the FRIENDLY animals there.

PANGY, THE SHY PANGOLIN

By S. Varalakshmi

It was night when Leon the Lion came running, muttering under his breath angrily.

"How dare they? How dare they?" He was also panting as he spoke.

Rasika the Rabbit heard him and asked, "What happened, Leon? You look angry."

Leon roared, "Of course I am angry. I found two poachers near the edge of the jungle trying to enter the forest when they spotted me and then ran away. I gave them a good chase and only when they drove off in their vehicle, I felt better."

"Poachers?" asked Rasika. "What did they want?"

"They were talking about a **pangolin**. Whatever that is!" said Leon.

MEETING A PANGOLIN

"Pangolins are shy, harmless mammals. They are also called scaly **ANTEATERS**. But they like to be left alone and are not found here in our jungle. I heard they are found somewhere near the Himalayan foothills, which is very far away," Rasika explained.

"Hmm... I haven't seen one. Have you, Rasika?" asked Leon curiously.

"No. But I am glad that you drove the poachers away. I guess they are gone forever," replied Rasika.

"I hope so," said someone softly from behind a bush.

Startled, Rasika and Leon looked around to find a strange animal, coming out of the bush towards them.

"Who are you? We have never seen you here before," asked Leon.

"I am the pangolin who you were just talking about. My name is Pangy. I am looking for a safe place to live in India, away from poachers," she introduced herself shyly.

Excited, Rasika and Leon introduced themselves to Pangy.

They then noticed a baby pangolin riding on Pangy's tail.

Following their eyes, Pangy introduced her baby with a tender smile, "That's my two-month-old baby that we call a **pangopup**. I named her Pi."

Rasika and Leon smiled **affectionately** at Pi as she clutched onto her mother, looking at them.

After a while, Bobby the Bear who was looking for Rasika saw him talking to Pangy and Leon. He greeted them all.

“Hello, Rasika. Hello, Leon. Who is your new friend?” asked Bobby curiously.

Turning around, Rasika introduced Pangy. “Hello, Bobby, meet Pangy pangolin and her daughter Pi. They are new around here.”

PANGY INTRODUCES HERSELF

Bobby smiled at Pangy and Pi. “Pleased to meet you both. Where are you from, Pangy?” he asked,

“I am from Africa, even though some of my relatives live in parts of Asia,” replied Pangy.

“Wow! Interesting. So how do you like Sundervan?” asked Bobby who could not stop himself from asking Pangy one question after another.

“I like it here. Rasika and Leon have been kind and friendly,” she said and smiled.

“Well, please add me to the list of being your friend,” said Bobby, with a grin. Pangy smiled and nodded.

"Hey, your **scales** look more beautiful than mine!" Boomed a loud voice.

They all turned to see Caleb the Crocodile, walking towards them, admiring Pangy.

Pangy delighted with the **compliment**, said, "Thank you. My scales are made of **KERATIN**, which is the same **PROTEIN** found in the hair and nails of human beings. Though our scales make us look beautiful, they are also a curse for our **SPECIES** as we are hunted for them. Our scales are used in making traditional Chinese medicines. We are also hunted for our meat, which is considered to be a delicacy in China and Vietnam."

"How sad! Even I am poached for my skin! So, you see, you are not alone. Even the great Caleb is hunted by the

poachers," grinned Caleb.

"Caleb! How can you joke and feel proud about it?" said Rasika horrified.

"Sorry, Rasika and Pangy. I simply wanted to tell Pangy that even I am part of an **endangered** species which is hunted for its skin."

"What does endangered mean?" asked Leon who had been quietly listening to everyone.

"Endangered means that only a few of us are left on Earth, and our species will not remain if humans don't stop hunting us," explained Pangy.

GETTING TO KNOW PANGY

"Pangy, how do you escape from **PREDATORS** in that case? You look so harmless. Not like me, with big teeth and a strong tail," asked Caleb.

"Well, when threatened, we roll ourselves into a tight ball protecting our soft belly and babies with our scales. We let out a **stinky fluid** from a **gland** at the base of our tails as a defence that makes our predator run away," Pangy explained.

"Sounds great! We would love to invite you to dinner if you let us know what you like to eat?" asked Rasika.

"Thank you for the invitation, Rasika. We feast on ants and termites," said Pangy.

Surprised, Bobby asked, "But how is that possible?"

"Pangolins, have long **SNOUTS** and even longer tongues, which we use to reach ants and termites that we excavate from mounds with our powerful front **claws**. We close our noses and ears to keep ants out while we are eating," said Pangy.

Leon yawned and said, "I am tired. Don't you all feel like turning in?"

"Pangolins are NOCTURNAL so I feel wide awake. I will return to my burrow later," said Pangy.

Caleb joked, "Guess you are like a nightguard, huh?"

"Along with the owls," said Pangy.

Pi made a sound which drew Pangy's attention.

"Why don't you invite your relatives here to live with us, Pangy? We would love for you to stay with us. This forest is very safe from poachers," said Leon.

Pangy smiled and nodded her head. "Of course, you are all very kind and friendly. I will write to my relatives and invite them here. Pi loves it already as I can see from the EXPRESSION on her face."

"Hey, shall we all take a SELFIE with our new friend and her baby?" asked Rasika.

"Though I am shy, I would love to send this photo to my relatives in Africa to invite them here," replied Pangy.

They all smiled and took a selfie, for a friendship that they hope would last forever!

EMAIL FROM SANTA CLAUS

By Inderjeet Kaushik

Barty the Bear had saved every single penny to buy a new **smartphone**. Now that he had finally bought it, he couldn't take his mind off it.

But he did not know how to use it and kept pressing random buttons.

AN EXCITING EMAIL

'Ting Ting!' the notification tone on his mobile rang. Barty touched the **icon** and opened the **EMAIL**. It said, 'Email from

Santa Claus.' Since Barty couldn't read, he did not understand the text written in it.

He went to his friend and asked her to read it to him. "Wow! It seems like LUCK has finally started favouring you. It is an email from Santa Claus and it says that because of his ill health, he will not be able to DISTRIBUTE gifts to everybody. Instead, he has decided to directly transfer money to the accounts of those on his 'Nice' list. And you are one of them!" she said, reading the email.

Barty jumped with joy when he heard this. "Let me go to Champakvan Bank and withdraw this money immediately and then we can celebrate our CHRISTMAS lavishly," he said and left.

BARTY GOES TO THE BANK

"I wish to withdraw the ₹50,000 deposited in my account," Barty said to the clerk sitting at the cash counter.

The clerk took his details and checked the account statement and politely said, "Sir, your account has ₹1000 in it. There are no new deposits."

"That's not true! You don't know how to do your job; let me talk to your manager instead," said Barty angrily, and STOMPED his way to the manager's cabin.

"Sir, how can I help you?" asked the manager. An angry Barty demanded to withdraw the ₹50,000 deposited in his account.

"But your account does not have that much money; you could be mistaken," the manager said, while cross-checking Barty's account.

Barty couldn't believe it. He then showed the manager the email he had received from **Santa Claus**.

"Tell me, why can't you give me the ***MONEY*** that Santa Claus has deposited in my account?" asked Barty angrily.

"Now I understand," said the bank manager. "Mr Barty, such messages or emails are usually **fake**. I would suggest you ignore them lest you may suffer a great loss in the future," he explained and got back to his work.

Barty did not want to leave the bank without his money and stood there hoping to get the matter solved. Jason the Jackal, who was in the bank, had been **OBSERVING** Barty for quite some time.

A SCAM?

"Barty, I heard what you just said. The people in this bank do not want to work. I will get you your money if you come with me," said Jason.

Barty was **CONFIDENT** that Santa Claus gifted him the money, so he immediately agreed to go along with Jason.

"Before you, others had come to Champakvan Bank to get their money but then realised that it was the wrong bank. Their money had been deposited in the new Forest Bank. Let us go there," said Jason. Barty went along.

They reached Forest Bank and met with the **MANAGER** to get Barty's money.

"To withdraw the ₹50,000, you have to open an account in this bank. You need to deposit ₹10,000 to open a new account," said the manager, Ajay the Anteater.

Barty did not have ₹10,000 and wasn't sure what to do. He got an idea and went to his friend Leo the Leopard to **BORROW** the money and promised Leo that he would return the money the next day.

Barty went back to the bank and gave Ajay ₹10,000. Once the account was opened, he impatiently said, "Give me my ₹50,000 now please."

"Sir, did you not read the account opening **DOCUMENTS**? The **POLICY** states that you cannot withdraw the money immediately. You have to wait for a day. Come tomorrow and we will have your ₹50,000 ready for you," said Ajay.

"How can I trust that you will give me my money?" asked Barty, now a little **suspicious**, especially as he couldn't read the documents he signed.

"We are Santa's helpers. This money has come to you as a Christmas gift from Santa, so if we don't give it to you, he will find and punish us," said Jason.

"You should go home without any worry. You will definitely get your **money** tomorrow," added Ajay. Barty believed them and went home **happily** to share the news.

A PAINFUL OUTCOME

The next day Barty went to Forest Bank, but it was **shut**. He looked around but there was no sign of Jason the Jackal and Ajay the Anteater.

Barty had been **ROBBED** not only of his gift of ₹50,000 but also of the ₹10,000 that he had borrowed from Leo.

The following day, Leo walked into Barty's house and roared for his money back. Barty explained that he would return Leo's money in **PARTS** as he had to sell some of his **BELONGINGS** to pay him back.

As Barty was talking to Leo, there was another notification on his mobile. 'Email from Santa Claus'! The new message offered a gift of ₹1,00,000 instead of ₹50,000.

Barty now realised that these messages were to make fools of people and rob them of their money.

DECODE THE CODE PUZZLE TIME

A message has been delivered from Santa Claus. Can you decode it?

      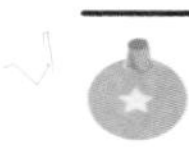 

       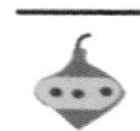 

 =C  = M  =O  = A = T

=I =W =N  =S  = G

* Answer on the last page

FRUITS OF LABOUR

"Hey! Small fry, get over here!" said Sam the Crab to Jai the Crab when Jai scuttled (a style of walking sideways, unique to crabs) past.

"Only baby fish are called fry," said Jai. "I'm a CRAB and what do you want?"

"Whatever, it's not important," said Sam. "Listen, I have an offer for you. Do my work and I will give you my PASTRY."

"What kind of work?" asked Jai, a little curious yet cautious.

"Go and get me a bottle of shell polish from the market."

"Shell polish? What is that?"

RICHER BY A PASTRY?

"My mistake, I forgot you are from the deep sea. See, shell polish is to make my outer body shiny. Now go and bring me some shell polish!"

"Why don't you go get it yourself?" asked Jai, a little insulted. "You should learn to do your work on your own!"

"This little crab from the deep sea lectures me on what to do and what not to do? Fine, go away! I'll get some other crab to bring me some shell polish!" said Sam and caught another passing crab. With Sam's offer sounding like a fair trade, the other crab agreed to go buy some shell polish in exchange for the pastry.

"Did you see that?" asked Sam snugly. "How happy he was when I offered him a pastry for bringing me some shell polish? Too bad you missed your chance."

"It's not always a good thing to get your work done through others," said Jai. "Keep this up and you're going to become lazy!"

"What's the point in taking so much effort when I can pay money for somebody else to do my work for me?" asked Sam counting the money in his FAT wallet.

"A wise man once said, 'There is no substitute for—"

"Listen, I don't have time for your stories," said Sam, cutting Jai off. "If you had spent less time lecturing me and more time bringing me my shell polish, you would have been richer by a pastry!"

MONEY OVER FOOD

Sam handed over the pastry to the little crab who had returned from the market and opened his bottle of shell POLISH.

'I don't want your free pastry', said Jai and scuttled away.

"Hahaha! I seem to have upset him! Maybe I should have given him a pastry anyway! Let me know if you're in need of work kid! I have plenty of work and plenty of rewards!" Sam shouted, making fun of Jai.

Gradually, Sam became lazier and lazier. He did not step out from his reef at all and if he needed any work done, he got somebody else to do it for him.

Over time, Sam grew fat from eating all day and not working at all. All the crabs in the reef, tempted by his sweets and

pastries, became Sam's workers except for Jai. One day, as Jai was returning from the neighbouring REEF he suddenly heard the sound of someone crying.

When he saw no one around, Jai asked aloud, "Who's there? Who's crying?"

"It's me, in the seaweed," said a familiar voice.

"Sam, what are you doing here?"

"Jai, we will talk later, first free me from this net. I am caught!"

"What are you saying Sam, you're trapped in a net? Why don't you just cut yourself free with your CLAWS? It should be an easy thing for even the tiniest of crabs!"

"Maybe you're right, but it's been a while since I actually used my claws for such work. They're not as sharp as they used to be and I'm just not able to cut through!" said Sam pitifully.

"Amazing, I never thought this was even remotely possible', muttered Jai to himself.

"Stop staring and cut me free, will you?" said Sam irritated. "The harder I try to squirm free, the tighter the net gets around me. Cut me loose please!" Jai cut him free and Sam heaved a sigh of relief.

"Oh, now I am alive again!" Sam said breathing heavily.

FRIENDS FINALLY

'Forgive me Jai, you were right. We should do our own work. I became so lazy getting others to work for me that today when I was trapped, I could not even cut myself free. I don't know what would have happened if you hadn't come to my rescue! Jai, will you forgive me?" asked Sam, realising his mistake.

"Of course, dear friend," said Jai, giving Sam a tight HUG.

A lesson was learnt and all was forgotten as the two friends scuttled back to their reef.

THE FLYING ELEPHANT

By Inderjeet Kaushik

As soon as Manny the Monkey rode down the street on his bicycle, all the animals stared at him. While a monkey on a bicycle was not an odd thing on its own, Manny was unique to look at because of all the colourful **balloons** tied to his bicycle.

BABY RABBITS LEARN TO FLY

When the little rabbits who lived down the street heard the sound of Manny's bell, they became very excited. Dropping their TOYS, they ran towards Manny and surrounded him. One by one, with their pocket money, they bought Manny's balloons when suddenly they heard...

"Help me! I'm taking off!" cried Minnie the tiniest rabbit of them all. "I'm small and the balloon is taking me with it. Help me, or I'll fly away!"

As Manny was trying to help Minnie down, the other rabbits decided to copy Minnie. "Wow! These balloons are amazing! With these, we could fly around the world!" they said and quickly bought the rest of Manny's balloons.

They tied the balloons around their waists. The smaller ones took off with just one balloon while the bigger ones took off with two or three.

Seeing this, Manny began to panic. "These balloons are filled with HELIUM!" He cried. "It will take you up nice and easy, but how do you plan on getting back down?"

ELLIE TO THE RESCUE

But no one paid attention to his words and one by one they began to float up. They were too high up for Manny to jump up and grab. He quickly ran to Ellie the Elephant. "Ellie! Ellie! You have to help me!" he cried and told her the whole story.

"I will definitely help you," said Ellie. "But you need to promise me one thing. Promise me that you will then use your balloons and make me float in the air!" Manny hastily agreed and the two set off to the playground where the rabbits were floating and having fun.

Ellie reached out with her trunk and pulled the baby rabbits down one by one and Manny untied the balloons from the rabbits and tied them back onto his CYCLE.

When all the rabbits were safely back on the ground, it was time for Manny to keep his promise and make Ellie fly! One by one he tied the balloons to Ellie's trunk, ears, body and tail. He was completely out of balloons but Ellie's feet were still firmly planted on the ground.

"This is the last one Ellie," said Manny. "I've got no more balloons left for you. I guess elephants were never meant to fly." Saying this, he got on his bicycle and zipped off.

THE TERRIBLE TANTRUM

Ellie felt sad and then became angry. Ever since she was a little girl, she always wanted to fly. She wanted to feel the **wind** in her ears and catch **clouds** with her trunk. Now that her dream was not going to be fulfilled, she decided to throw a **tantrum**.

She walked into a busy intersection. She blocked cars, buses and lorries and the traffic was soon backed up in all directions. An angry car driver asked her to stop blocking the traffic.

"I'm not going to move!" She said FIRMLY, her balloons SWAYING left and right in the wind. "Until I float off the ground, I'm not moving!"

A crowd gathered around Ellie and among them was Roro the Rabbit. Roro immediately realised that this wouldn't end well if Ellie continued to stay in that spot. Ellie was in the middle of a train crossing and in just a few minutes the Jungle Express would be coming their way.

ELLIE FINALLY GETS HER WISH

Realising that there might not be enough time to make Ellie understand the seriousness of the situation, Roro began to look around. She got an idea and knew just how to save Ellie. Just a few days ago when it had rained, a truck had tipped over nearby on the slippery roads. A big CRANE had been called in to remove the truck and the crane was still there.

Roro quickly ran up to the crane operator and explained to him that the Jungle Express would be passing through the CITY in some time and Ellie was in the way. The crane operator quickly jumped into the crane and moved closer to Ellie.

Roro tied one end of a thick **ROPE** to the crane's hook and the other around Ellie. Ellie was lifted off the ground and she floated over the traffic to safety. Ellie's lifelong dream of flying finally came true. The crane operator swung her around gently for some time and then let her down.

Once on the ground, she quickly ran off to tell her friends about her amazing experience while everyone praised Roro for her presence of mind.

SHADOW MATCH

PUZZLE TIME

Ellie is excited after flying and is posing differently.
Match her shadows with her pose.

* Answer on the last page

BHIM AND THE BOOK THIEF

By Kunvar Premil

Bhim the Water Buffalo had the best house in the entire forest. It was nestled between tall, thick trees. Bhim's house was very special to him.

What was even more special about Bhim's house was his library. Filled end to end with beautiful books, the library was his prized possession. Any animal who happened to catch Bhim with a book, could see the happiness on his face.

BHIM'S BOOKS GO MISSING

One day, Bhim thought that the number of books in his library was decreasing. Realising that there may be a thief, he decided to become alert. Even then, Bhim's books kept decreasing.

After much thought, Bhim finally had a perfect idea. On the day before Holi, Bhim sprinkled some coloured powder at the entrance to the library. He thought that when the thief entered the library, he or she would step on the colour powder and surely leave his or her prints behind and get caught.

As expected, Bhim found a set of paw prints all over the library floor. From the PRINTS, he realised that a hyena was the book thief. Bhim knew exactly who could the hyena be and who could help him out.

BHIM'S PLAN

The next day, Bhim walked up to Candy the Vixen and struck up a conversation. "Hi Candy! How are you? Come on; let's take a walk through the forest. I found a grapevine a few metres away. It has the biggest and juiciest grapes I have ever seen!"

"No way, Bhim," said Candy. "The **GRAPES** will definitely be sour. And, how do you plan on reaching them? I'm sure all the good ones are too high up on the vine."

"Don't worry Candy." said Bhim reassuringly. "You can climb up on my back and pluck the grapes from the vine. After that, we'll eat the grapes together!"

Candy, who had only tasted sour grapes all her life readily accepted Bhim's offer. They reached the grapevine and she quickly climbed up on Bhim's back and PLUCKED the grapes. She popped the grapes in her mouth one by one and shouted in delight, "These are the best grapes I have ever tasted!"

"I can help you with grapes just like these every day if you'd like!" said Bhim. "But you will have to do me one favour!"

CANDY SOLVES BHIM'S PROBLEM

That very night, with the help of her friends, Candy found out who the book thief was. She found Willy the Hyena curled up in his den with one of Bhim's books. Willy, it seemed had assembled a library of his own with Bhim's books. Candy knew just how to get the books back.

The next day was Holi and Candy's plan was already in motion. With all the little cubs, Candy set off towards Willy's den armed with water guns and colour powder.

They tiptoed into the house, and sneaked inside his room.

Willy was curled up in his bed between the sheets, completely engrossed in his book. He didn't realise that he was no longer alone. Candy and the cubs shouted "It's Holi! It's Holi! It's Holi!"

A FUN-FILLED HOLI

Willy saw Candy and the cubs with the water guns and leapt out of his bed with a shock. He ran like the wind, out of his room. Candy's plan had worked perfectly. She and the cubs moved the books one by one from Willy's to Bhim's house. By the end of the day, Bhim's library was back to its original state, filled with beautiful books.

Willy realised his mistake and apologised to Bhim. Bhim told him that he was welcome to borrow any book that he wanted to read. Saying so, Bhim picked up a bucket of water and drenched Willy shouting, "Happy Holi!" Candy, the cubs, Bhim and Willy ate the sweetest, juiciest, most delicious grapes together.

COMPLETE THE PICTURE

PUZZLE TIME

Like Bhim the Buffalo, Blacky the Bear also likes to read. Parts of this image have been left blank. Look at the picture, complete it and then colour it.

* Answer on the last page

JORAM

By Aman

There was excitement in Kalindi colony because a new family had just moved in—Mr Moseng the Baboon, his wife and their son Joram. The entire colony lined up to meet them and help them settle in.

The Mosengs were from AFRICA and Mr Moseng, who worked at a bank, had been transferred here. Soon, a week passed by and the Mosengs were settled in.

One evening, Joram's mother suggested, "Joram, why don't you go outside and play with the other animals?"

MAKING FRIENDS

Joram stepped outside and approached a group of cubs. When they saw Joram walking towards them, they all SURROUNDED him. They hadn't seen anyone who looked like him.

"Hi, my name is Joram. Can I play with you?" asked Joram feeling a little UNCOMFORTABLE.

"Why are you so tiny?" asked one of the cubs.

"I think he's a dwarf," said another.

"Look how long his SNOUT is," said the third.

"He looks so weird!"

"What did you say your name was again?" asked Fahad, one of the cubs.

"My name is Joram."

Immediately, Fahad started laughing and all the others joined in. Joram felt sad to see that they were laughing at him but remained **quiet**. After playing for some time, they all went back home.

The next day, Joram stepped out to play with the other animals in the colony. When Fahad saw him approach them, he began shouting "Look, the **WEIRDO** is here! Run!"

All the children ran away laughing and Joram was left all alone. Feeling sad, he went back home and stopped trying to be friends with anyone.

One evening, Fahad saw Joram eating bananas. He again made fun of him. When Joram saw everybody around him laughing he felt very sad and ran away.

JORAM HELPS FAHAD

One day, there was a **fair** at Kalindi colony. All the animals from the colony were having a great time playing on the **rides**. Fahad and his friends were on the **swing**, and Fahad slipped and fell. He was badly hurt.

Joram, who had seen this happen, immediately rushed to his help. He cleaned his wounds and took him to a doctor. Fahad was very surprised to see that Joram helped him even though he had been mean to him all this time.

FAHAD MAKES AMENDS

Fahad told his grandfather about how Joram had helped him despite him giving Joram a tough time. His grandfather explained, "Just because Joram looks different doesn't mean he is less than you or that you should make fun of him. Maybe, you would now like to thank him for helping you when you were in need."

"But will he accept my APOLOGY?" asked Fahad.

"You will only know once you go and apologise."

Fahad's grandfather accompanied him to Joram's house. Joram forgave Fahad in an instant and gave him a big hug. From that day on, the two of them became the best of friends.

THE NAUGHTY DUCKLING

By Ilika Priy

Dolly the Duck would always be thinking of ways to fool others. Her mother Milly would try to get her to stop but it was of no use. Nothing stopped her from playing pranks on others.

One day, there was a festival in the area. The other ducks and ducklings were celebrating it by bursting crackers, playing with coloured powders, singing and DANCING on the streets.

Milly had bathed all the ducklings, and now it was her turn. "Sit here quietly and wait for me. Don't step outside. Everybody is playing with colours and you don't want to get any of that stuff on you," she said.

While all her brothers and sisters sat patiently inside, Dolly couldn't control herself. She ran outside to take part in the festivities.

A RED DUCKLING

Dolly walked amongst the other ducks who were celebrating with colours.

She saw a big drum. Wondering what was in it, she climbed to the top of the DRUM and **peered** inside. Suddenly, she lost her balance and fell into the drum.

She jumped out right away, but it was too late—her feathers were DYED red. She began to shiver in the cold air.

When she looked at her wings, she was shocked, “If my wings are red, that means, my entire body is red too!” Excited, she walked back to her house.

DOLLY PLAYS A PRANK

When Dolly reached her **neighbourhood**, all the other ducklings stopped playing and stared at her. They had never seen such a colourful duckling before.

"Who is this? I've never seen her before. Where did she come from?" the ducklings whispered to each other. Dolly was **thrilled** when she heard this because it gave her an idea for another **PRANK**.

"I wonder what's happening at home?" thought Dolly. "Maybe I'll go later because I don't want mummy to **recognise** me and spoil my fun," she said to herself.

Dolly **wandered** around the neighbourhood fooling all the other ducklings. After a while, she got **bored** of the game and headed home.

BACK HOME

When she reached, she saw all her brothers, sisters and mother. "They have no idea it's me. This is going to be so much **fun**!" he thought to herself.

Dolly went to her brother, Abdul and asked, "What's the matter? Why are you so worried?"

"Our sister Dolly is missing. We haven't seen her all morning. Who are you?" asked Abdul.

"I am from the future," Dolly said and **fooled** Abdul into thinking she was a **ROBOT**.

Then she went up to her mother,

"What's the matter, ma'am? Who are you looking for?" she asked.

"My daughter Dolly has been missing all day. The poor thing hasn't eaten anything since morning. I hope she's safe," she said **worriedly**.

All the MISCHIEVOUS thoughts in Dolly's head disappeared and her eyes began to well up with tears. Here she was having fun and making a fool of everybody while her mother was worried sick.

She was just about to tell her that it was her covered in red colour, when Milly said, "Why don't you go inside and eat something. I'll go look for Dolly."

A MOTHER'S LOVE

Reluctantly she said, "Mummy, it's me, Dolly. I'm right here. I fell in a drum of red-coloured water."

"Oh my, it is you! Are you ok? Are you hurt? Are you feeling cold? Where did you fall? How did it happen?" asked Milly, picking Dolly up and holding her close.

Dolly was now Confused. She expected her mother to SCOLD her at the least. "Mummy takes such good care of me, I will try to never give her so much grief again," thought Dolly.

Dolly gave Milly a big hug and **promised** to be less naughty in the future. She learned that no prank will make her feel as good as being HUGGED by her mother.

COMPLETE THE PICTURE

PUZZLE TIME

Parts of this image have been left blank. Look at the picture, complete it and then colour it.

THE NEW NEIGHBOUR

By Ilika Priy

Ricky the Sheep loved playing detective. He would always be SNEAKING around looking for clues. Since he never got into any serious trouble, he wouldn't listen when other animals asked him to stop snooping around.

One day Ricky's friend, Dipti said, "Hey Ricky, have you met our new neighbour? He is a big, strong wolf, but he is a really nice guy. I just met him."

Ricky said, "Oh that's nice," but he wasn't convinced. He had never heard of a wolf being kind to sheep. He decided to INVESTIGATE by sneaking into the wolf's home.

RICKY DECIDES TO POKE AROUND

That night, Ricky decided that it was safe to enter the wolf's home. He walked up to the front door, trying to be as quiet as possible when suddenly the door opened and out came Wayne the Wolf.

"Hi neighbour!" said Wayne, warmly. Ricky got startled by his sudden appearance and ran away.

"I wonder what's up with him," said Wayne and went back inside.

"Oh! I shouldn't have gone through the main door," thought Ricky. "I will need to find another way to get in."

The next night when the whole forest was asleep, Ricky got out of bed and walked up to Wayne's house. He circled to the back of the house and climbed onto the roof.

As Ricky was about to drop down into the house through the SKYLIGHT, Wayne shouted from below.

"Aren't you the sheep from last night? What are you doing up there?" he asked.

Hearing Wayne's voice, Ricky's **FLEECE** stood on end. Ricky quickly climbed down the roof and ran away.

"I better keep an eye out for that one," Wayne muttered to himself.

RICKY ENTERS THROUGH THE CHIMNEY

Ricky ran straight to his house and took a deep breath. "That was close," he thought to himself. "I must find a safer way to sneak in."

For two days Ricky made no move. Soon, he had a plan and was ready to investigate again. "Why not enter the house from the chimney?" thought Ricky.

He waited in the bushes until all the lights went out. When it seemed like the wolf was finally asleep, he quickly climbed up onto the roof and slid down the **CHIMNEY**. He landed on something soft and suddenly, everything

became very dark.

"I've got you now you thief!" said Wayne and quickly raised an alarm. All the sheep in the area came running.

When the lid was opened, Ricky realised that he had been trapped in a chest full of blankets.

"This sheep has been trying to sneak into my house. We must arrest him. Call the police!" said Wayne.

The rest of the sheep explained that Ricky meant no harm, but did not trust that any wolf could be nice to sheep, so he had started his own investigations on Wayne. Hearing this, Wayne calmed down.

"You should be careful Ricky," said Wayne. "You were

fortunate that your friends could rescue you. Imagine what would have happened if they weren't here to save you?"

"Trust me," Wayne added. "I really mean no harm. Because of my health problems, doctors have advised that I lead a simple life and not eat meat. Since FRUITS and vegetables aren't easily available where I lived before, I moved here."

"You are welcome inside my home at any time Ricky. Just try knocking first," Wayne said, and all the sheep started laughing.

Ricky learnt two valuable lessons that night. One, that snooping and sneaking weren't good things. The other was that it is wrong to make assumptions about others before meeting them.

SPOT THE DIFFERENCE

Circle 10 differences you can find between the two pictures.

MICE IN A CAGE

By Manoj Roy

Cindy the Cat had just come back from the city, and she had completely changed. She wore a fancy hat, a pair of dark sunglasses and a bright pink suit.

All the other cats at Kittyville surrounded her. "Where have you been?" "You look so stylish!" "Were you at the city?" they asked.

"Call me aunty," said Cindy. "I was in the city. I had a **FASHION** show there and just got back."

A NEW GIZMO

"Aunty, what did you get us from the city?" asked Gail the Kitten.

"A mouse cage trap," said Cindy.

"A mouse cage trap?" the other cats **murmured** amongst themselves.

“With this, chasing mice is a thing of the past. All you need to do is put some food on the hook inside. When a mouse enters and pulls on the piece of food, the door slams shut, and the mouse is trapped,” explained Cindy.

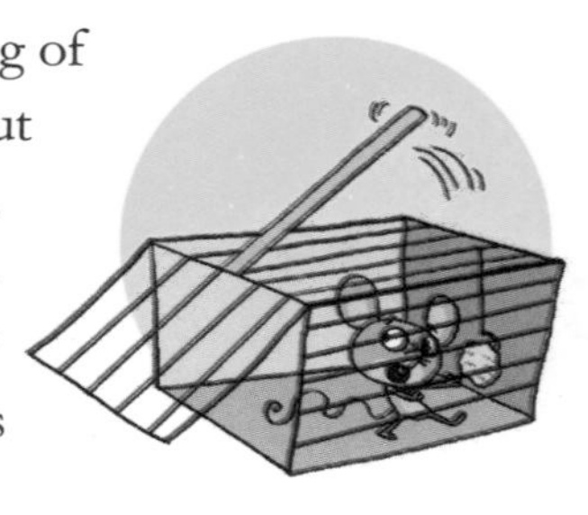

“That’s amazing!” exclaimed Minnie the Cat.

“I’ve brought enough for everybody and it can be yours for the tiny sum of ₹1000, only,” said Cindy pulling more traps from her car.

Soon, all the cats began using the mouse traps to catch mice. Wherever they would see a burrow, they would leave a piece of bread in the mousetrap and place it nearby. The mice being simple-minded would get caught.

THE MICE BAND TOGETHER

Seeing the number of mice in the area disappearing, Manny the Mouse decided to bring all the mice together for a meeting.

“Brothers and sisters, you must be aware of the **TRAP** Cindy has distributed among all the other cats. We need to get the word across to all the mice that they need to avoid the trap at all costs," said Manny.

"But how?" asked Jimbo the Mouse rubbing his fat tummy. "We are mice. If we see food, we jump at it immediately."

"We have begun maintaining a stockpile of food in the **BURROWS**," said Pinky the Mouse. From now on, the only thing we must worry about is not getting trapped.

Soon, all the mice thought twice before approaching any food placed inside a cage. The cats were very unhappy about this.

A NEW PRODUCT

With the cats no longer needing to chase after mice, they had all grown fat. They would grow short of breath very quickly. They realised that their lives were much better before Cindy brought them the traps.

"I have a solution to this," said Cindy. "The problem is that you have all grown fat. But I have a special TEA that I brought back from the city. If you drink it for a month, you'll be as SLIM as me and it costs ₹1000, only!"

The cats may have fallen into her trap before, but they weren't going to this time. They all ran after her and chased her away back to the CITY.

A TALE OF TWO FRIENDS

By Lalit Shaurya

Rexy the Rabbit was extremely proud of his golden blonde fur. He loved his long whiskers, too. Filled with pride, he didn't like to speak to the other animals of Anandvan. He felt they were all beneath him. And that is why he didn't have any friends.

Pip the Porcupine, on the other hand, was just the opposite. He was sweet and kind, and everyone in the forest loved him. He helped and respected everyone around him and had many friends. He liked to make new friends and even tried being friends with Rexy who always ignored him.

PIP TURNS DOWN REXY'S REQUEST

One day, Pip saw Rexy walking and he called out to him and said, "Hello, Rexy. How are you? Would you like to celebrate Friendship Day with me?"

"I have told you many times not to disturb me. I do not wish to talk to anyone in Anandvan, let alone you," Rexy said with irritation.

"What is it, Rexy? I just want us to be FRIENDS and what could be better way than Friendship Day?" said Pip.

"Friendship? With you? Never! Have you ever looked at yourself? Go and check your reflection in the pond and then think if you can be my friend," insulted Rexy.

"What does friendship have to do with how I look? Looks do not matter in friendship, hearts do. I know we can be good friends," said Pip, not losing hope.

"I do not wish to be friends with you. Look at my golden fur and my lovely WHISKERS and look at yourself! You carry a forest of thorns on your body. Who would want to be your friend?" Rexy continued to insult Pip.

"I have nothing else to say. You consider looks to be more important in friendship, so be it. You only want to have good-looking friends so forget I asked," said Pip and walked away.

PIP TO THE RESCUE

Rexy hopped away without giving it another thought. His words hurt Pip, but since Pip knew Rexy's nature, he tried not to feel hurt by what he said.

That same evening while Pip was walking along the riverbank, he heard someone's cries. It was coming from the bushes near the RIVER.

Pip quickly ran towards the sound. He was taken aback by what he saw there. Fred the Fox was holding Rexy in his claws, ready to eat him.

Pip attacked Fred with his sharp QUILLS, making him lose his grip on Rexy who fell and Fred ran away groaning in pain.

Pip's sharp quills had bruised him badly.

Rexy was in a state of shock. His throat was dry. Pip immediately brought some water from the river and gave it to him.

Rexy felt better, but realised how mean he had been to Pip. He felt ashamed and couldn't look Pip in the eye. He was sobbing.

THE BEGINNING OF A NEW FRIENDSHIP

"What is it Rexy? Why are you crying? Everything is fine now. Fred is gone and you are safe," Pip comforted Rexy.

"I said such harsh things to you in the morning and made fun of your looks. I even rejected your offer of friendship, but you still saved my life. I was mean and did not understand the true meaning of friendship. I am not worthy of your friendship," said Rexy with **REGRET**.

"You may have been mean to me but I know, you're still capable of being good. I think, whatever happens, happens for the best, so forget what you said in the morning and let's start afresh. We can be friends now," said Pip with a smile.

Rexy hugged Pip. He apologised for his behaviour once again. Pip took out a friendship band and gave it to Rexy who wore the band happily. The two friends wished each other a Happy Friendship Day

MAZE

Rexy the Rabbit has new friends. Help him reach them.

* Answer on the last page

BRINGING THE HOUSE DOWN

By Jamshed Azmi

Bobo the Bear lived in the jungle with his two brothers Barty and Bunty. While his brothers worked hard in the city every day, Bobo was as lazy as they were hard-working. He had a lot of belief in LUCK and felt that one day he would strike gold and become rich. He spent all daydreaming of riches.

Seeing him laze around all day, Barty said, "Bobo, you sit around all day doing nothing. Why don't you come with us to the city? We'll help you find a job. If you sit around all day, you'll never be independent."

"No Barty, I don't want to come. I don't have any real skills needed for a job and working with my hands is beneath me," said Bobo.

"Work is worship, Bobo. There should be no such thing as a job that's beneath you," said Bunty.

"Plus, if you start working, then some more MONEY will come into this house and we can live in more comfort," said Barty.

"I can't do such things," said Bobo. "I have lines of fortune on my palm, which show that I will one day find the treasure which will change my fate."

"Bobo, we are getting late for work. Try to spend your time doing something productive instead of daydreaming," said Barty and left with Bunty. Bobo filled his tummy with honey and lay down in his bed.

One day, when he was walking through the jungle, he came across a saint dressed in long, flowing CLOTHES with a kettle in his hand. Bobo went closer and asked who he was and where he had come from as he had never seen him before.

"My son, you are pretty sharp. This is the first time in many years in the SNOW-CAPPED peaks of the Himalayas. My name is Baba Chaturanand. How can I help you?" he asked Bobo.

"*Babaji*, could you please read my palm and tell me what my future is going to be like?" asked Bobo with hesitation.

"Of course," said Baba Chaturanand. "I am well versed in all forms of astrology, especially in palmistry. But for each reading, I charge a fee of ₹1000."

"Then I'd better be on my way, as I have only ₹500 with me," said Bobo feeling disappointed.

Baba Chaturanand stroked his beard and said after a deep sigh, "While I would normally never reduce my fee by even a rupee, seeing that your heart is pure, I shall read your palm for ₹500."

"Here you go, Babaji," said Bobo giving him the money. "Please tell me, when will fortunes shine upon me?"

Baba Chaturanand pocketed the **money** with one hand and took Bobo's hand in the other. He studied Bobo's palm with great concentration and said, "My child, your fortunes will change sooner than you might think. You will become the richest bear in the jungle."

"Really?" asked Bobo. "Where will I find this treasure?"

"In a few days, the location of this fortune will be revealed to you in a dream. You must be patient till then," said the Baba.

Bobo was delighted to hear that his luck is about to change. He touched the Baba's feet and went home with a skip in his step.

Bobo spent the next few days dreaming of the buried **treasure**. He couldn't wait for the location of the treasure to be revealed to him in the dream.

One night, he finally had the dream. He dreamt that the treasure was buried right under their house. To find the treasure, he would have to dig three feet under the house.

When he opened his eyes, it was morning. Barty and Bunty were yet to leave for work. While brushing his teeth, Bobo decided that the ideal time to dig would be when his brothers had left for work.

"When I dig the treasure out, I'll share it with my brothers and we will use the money to rebuild our house," thought Bobo.

As he was making BREAKFAST for himself, his brothers left for work. Bobo was very excited and could hardly control himself. Armed with a shovel, he began digging under and around the house. By noon, he had dug up the land around the house. He was so intent on finding the treasure that he didn't realise that he was covered in sweat.

When he realised that it wasn't outside the house, he began digging inside the house too. He finally stopped when he saw the entire floor was three feet deeper than it was before.

"It doesn't seem to be under the house. But the Babaji said that the location will be revealed in my dream. Maybe it's in the walls. I'll break them down and take a look before Bunty and Barty come back," he said to himself and got to it.

He broke down the last WALL when the entire roof caved in on him. The heavy roof knocked him down and he wasn't able to get up. He just lay there under the roof. He tried calling out for help, but nobody heard him.

In about two hours, Barty and Bunty came back home and were shocked to see their home in ruins.

"Oh no, how did this happen?" asked Barty.

"The house was fine till this morning. And where's Bobo?" asked Bunty.

"I'm here, under the roof," came a voice. It was Bobo's.

Barty and Bunty quickly started pushing bits of the **roof** aside and finally found Bobo.

"Bobo, what has happened to our home? Why were you under the roof?" they asked.

When Bobo narrated the entire story, his brothers were left speechless for a while.

"Do you realise that our entire home has been destroyed? Where are we going to live now?" they asked.

Barty and Bunty told Bobo that one's life doesn't change overnight and that success required lots of hard work. He and his brothers spent the next few months sleeping outside. But Bobo finally changed his ways. He worked hard and eventually became successful.

THE TEN-GRAM WEAKLING

By Kumud Kumar

It was during the SUMMER holidays when the animals of Sundarvan had the most fun. They spent all day playing, and at night, they'd all gather under the stars and dream. Their books had been packed away in their cupboards and no one was in a hurry to take them out.

While some animals went to hill stations to beat the heat with their families, others came to Sundarvan to meet their grandparents. In the evenings, the playground was always full.

The animals who loved playing cricket wanted to play something new. Elmo the Elephant suggested that they play **FOOTBALL**. "It's a lot of fun and we end up running around quite a lot too," he said.

Everyone liked Elmo's idea and they pooled their allowances together to buy a brand new football.

Now, they could hardly wait to play. When the game began, they all ran behind the ball. The ball went all over the ground. It went to the left, it went to the right, it sailed over their heads and it rolled on the ground. The animals never had so much fun before.

A NEW FRIEND

Sammy the Dormouse was a new visitor to Sundarvan. He had come to meet his grandparents.

Since he was new, he was still a stranger. But because he loved playing football so much, not having friends didn't stop him from going to the playground every evening.

Sammy tried hard to make friends and play with the other animals, but since he was a tiny dormouse, all the others thought he was a weakling and ignored him.

"Elmo, I want to play football. Please let me play on your team," requested Sammy.

"You want to play football? You're about as big as the football. What will you do? And if you come under somebody's feet, you'll be flattened like a papad," laughed Elmo, denying him a chance to play.

Hearing Elmo's remarks, all the other animals burst into LAUGHTER. Sammy, went home feeling sad.

The new football was extra bouncy and everyone would kick it really hard. One day when Elmo kicked the ball, it sailed over the playground's compound wall and landed in a DEEP pond.

The animals ran after the football and saw it in the middle of the pond. None of them dared to jump in. Not only was the pond deep, but it was also home to Crocky the Crocodile. He was mean-tempered and had called the POLICE on lots of animals who had mistakenly wandered into his pond.

Crocky waited for someone to come and pick up the football so that he could catch them and call the police.

THE TEN-GRAM WEAKLING

Sammy reached the pond and realised that this was the perfect opportunity to show the other animals that he was not weak. All the other animals made fun of him by calling him a 'Ten-gram weakling.'

Sammy ignored them and started his warm-up exercises. Then, he walked up to the water's edge and dove in like an experienced SWIMMER. The animals were shocked to see that Sammy had the courage to dive into Crocky's pond.

Sammy's dive put him pretty close to the centre of the pond and soon, he was near the ball. Crocky quickly swam towards Sammy. All the animals were worried. But Sammy wasn't. He knew just how to escape from a CROCODILE.

As Crocky gained in on Sammy, he dove down and hid behind Crocky who could not see him because he was so small.

The football was stuck among some lotus flowers. Sammy climbed on the lotus leaves and then on top of the ball. The animals began to cheer. When Crocky saw Sammy standing on top of the football, he was FURIOUS. With great force, he whacked the ball with his tail.

Both Sammy and the football sailed over the water and landed near the shore. The animals quickly rescued Sammy and cheered him.

The next evening, everybody wanted Sammy on their TEAM. Nobody called him a weakling and he played football with them every day.

That day, Sammy learnt a very valuable lesson. He learnt that how people treat you is in your hands and unless you show them what you are capable of, they will never find out.

PICTURE STORY

PUZZLE TIME

The animals are having some summer fun. Look at the pictures below and arrange them in order to tell the story.

1

2

3

4

5

6

7

8

THE MANTIS PROBLEM

By Jamshed Azmi

In a school in a little town, there was a beautiful garden. The flowers that bloomed there got the most beautiful butterflies and the children had fun chasing the BUTTERFLIES around.

One day, a mantis happened to pass by. He saw the garden and decided to stick around. "This garden is so beautiful. The perfect place to spend the rest of my days," he said to himself.

MANTIS FINDS A HOME

He settled down in a COMFORTABLE bush and started a new life there. The next day, when the children came to the garden to have fun and play with the butterflies, he came out of his hiding place to watch.

This was when he was noticed. A boy happened to be walking past the mantis' bush when he saw him. "Guys, look, there's a mantis here," said the boy.

Having never seen a mantis before, all the children gathered to take a look. The mantis' bright green colour wowed the children.

JEALOUSY ARISES

All the attention they were giving him made the mantis think. "If all the children are giving me so much attention, it must mean that I am as beautiful as some of the butterflies. If I start getting rid of the more beautiful ones, then I can become the KING of this garden," he said to himself.

Later that day, when the children had all gone home and the garden was empty, the mantis set off to take care of **BUSINESS**. He found the butterflies with the brightest colours and the biggest wings and chased them away one by one.

One evening, when the mantis was **BULLYING** the butterflies into leaving the garden, Sanya the Butterfly asked, "Why are you so set on chasing us away? What have we ever done to you?"

"It's not about what you did to me; it's really about what I can do without you around. With no butterflies to **distract** the children, they will only look at me," said the mantis.

"You're going to **REGRET** it," said Mona, another butterfly.

The mantis grew WILD. “How dare you speak to me this way? I’ll teach you a thing or two about regrets,” he said and chased after them. Fearing their safety, the butterflies flew away from the garden and settled down in a nearby tree. They kept their activities to a minimum, afraid that they’d attract the mantis’s attention.

With the garden rid of butterflies, the mantis was the king. The children played with him and the mantis’s life was good.

THE BUTTERFLIES CONSIDER WHAT TO DO

As the butterflies watched this from their tree, a MONARCH butterfly stood up and said, “This is not right. How long will we live like this? Something has to be done.”

"You're right, we have to get rid of the mantis," agreed Mona.

"Then what are we waiting for? Let's go and take back what's rightfully ours," suggested the monarch butterfly.

Sanya took a deep breath. "Let's not rush this. A mantis has five eyes. Even if we try sneaking up on him, he'll see us for sure and the results could be disastrous for us. We need a plan," she said. "Just give me some time to think."

SANYA HAS AN IDEA

Sanya was lost in thought when she suddenly saw a group of children playing cricket. Soon, she had a plan. When she shared it with the rest, they couldn't contain their HAPPINESS.

Sanya flew down to the garden and had a chat with the mantis. "Hello, how are you doing?" she asked him.

"Forget about me, how are you doing? I hope you're alright. I haven't seen you around in these parts for so long... of course, that could be because I finally got rid of the butterflies," he said with an EViL laugh.

"Laugh all you want," said Sanya. "It's not going to last long."

"What do you mean?" asked the mantis, **annoyed**.

"While I don't see any point behind telling you this, I just thought you should know. The children are planning something and it's not going to end well for you. I just OVERHEARD them talking about how they want to get rid of you," she said.

"That's impossible," said the mantis. "The children ADORE me. They would never do anything to hurt me."

"Choose not to believe me if you wish. All I can say is that things aren't going to be too pretty if you decide to see for yourself. Just watch out for the tall kid," said Sanya and flew back to the tree.

The mantis was sure that nothing bad was going to happen. But the more he thought about it, the more worried he grew. He managed to CALM himself down and carry on with his day.

MANTIS FALLS FOR SANYA'S PLAN

When the SCHOOL BELL rang, like every other day, the children came to the garden. As the mantis basked in the sun, the children gathered around him and watched. Suddenly, the mantis noticed that a tall child was holding a stick in his hand. The mantis remembered what Sanya had said.

As the kid came closer, the mantis **panicked** and flew straight towards the child's face and **stung** him. The children realised that the mantis wasn't **friendly** anymore.

They caught him and threw him out of the garden. The butterflies were happy to see the mantis gone. They flew down from the tree and danced around the garden. They **thanked** Sanya for solving their problem.

A FRIGHTENING GHOST

By Ilika Priy

Malini jumped with joy when she noticed her egg crack.

"My baby is coming out of the egg," she shouted out to the neighbours.

In a little while, a CHICK came out of the SHELL and started touching Malini's beak with her tiny red beak. Malini's joy had no bounds. She gently **stroked** it back.

Spring was the season for the baby birds to hatch from eggs. From different branches of the trees came the *chi-chi* sound of baby sparrows.

Their parents were busy roaming the sky looking for food for the babies. All the parents loved

their NEWBORN babies a lot. Malini named her chick Bushra.

When she looked at her NEIGHBOUR, Lily with her child, she thought that she loved her baby more than other mothers loved their children.

When Malini and Lily went to bring food, their children Neelu and Bushra would chat together.

EXPLORING THE WORLD AROUND

One day Bushra said, "Neelu, see our feathers are growing. Now we should start hopping on the branches."

"Really? Then let's start hopping!" Neelu said, excited. And both of them came out of their NESTS.

"This is so much fun! I was thinking that the nest was our whole WORLD but the outside world is so beautiful!" Neelu said hopping around.

Both could see the green GRASS and colourful **flowers** down below from their high branch.

They were both hopping JOYFULLY from one branch to another when their mothers returned.

A MOTHER'S FEAR

Lily was very happy to see Neelu outside. But Malini was upset to see Bushra outside the nest.

"What are you doing out of the nest?" said Malini scolding her.

"See, mummy! I learned to hop. This is so much fun," Bushra said excitedly. She thought her mother would be happy with her achievement.

But Malini said angrily, "You are very small and you have to remain inside the nest."

"But it is so nice to hop," said Bushra, but Malini scolded her even more.

"Malini! Why are you getting so angry? The children are growing up. If they start hopping now, only then will they learn to fly tomorrow," said Lily.

Malini did not reply. She was afraid that if they hopped around like this, then some other bird would see and hurt them or that they would lose their balance and fall. So, she did not want Bushra to hop.

But Bushra did not listen to her mother and continued roaming with Neelu. Malini thought hard about how she could stop Bushra from getting out. Suddenly one day, she thought of a plan, "Ghost! A frightening ghost!"

BUSHRA LEARNS ABOUT GHOSTS

The next day, Malini said, "Bushra you must be wondering why I stop you from going out of the nest! It is because I am afraid that a ghost might catch you.

"A ghost? What is a ghost?" Bushra asked.

"A ghost is a very frightening thing! They have big teeth. They have neither legs nor wings. And they can **fly** in the air and catch anyone. They have **magical powers** and can eat anyone."

Bushra was terrified after hearing about **GHOSTS** from her mother. Malini now knew that Bushra would not go out of the nest. Now Bushra refused to go out of the nest, no matter how much Neelu called her.

THE AFTER EFFECT

In a few days, Neelu started taking small flights.

One day, Malini looked up in the SKY and saw small sparrows flying around. She could also spot Neelu among them. "When did these babies learn to fly?"

Lily smiled and said, "Neelu learnt to fly by hopping on the branches."

"But Bushra does not know how to fly!" Malini said SADLY.

"You don't allow Bushra to even hop. How would she learn to fly?" asked Lily.

Malini looked at her and said, "I was stopping her for her own safety."

"And your extreme safety made her weak. She has to get over her FEAR as we did. You did not give her a chance to learn anything," said Lily.

MALINI TRIES TO CORRECT HER ERROR

Malini realised her mistake. She asked Bushra to go out of the nest and hop around, but Bushra came back soon.

"Mummy, there may be a ghost outside. I am **afraid**," Bushra said slowly. Malini explained there was nothing outside. But Bushra came back again and said, "I feel frightened!"

Malini felt sad hearing this. Lily who saw all this, came over and said, "Malini, you have scared Bushra by putting the fear of a ghost in her. Children are like a blank camera. Whatever image you put in it that will remain there. It will take some time to wipe the fear off her mind. If you don't do it now, then she will believe in them all her life and will remain **SCARED**."

Now Malini realised her mistake and said, "You have opened my eyes, Lily. I thought fear will keep her safe but it has done more harm to her. I will try to take the fear out of her."

And Malini worked with Bushra and helped her **OVERCOME** her fear of ghosts. Soon Bushra started flying with Neelu in the sky, **UNDAUNTED**

I CAN

By Muraly TV

I don't think I can do it," Darryl the Donkey BRAYED loudly. Milo the Monkey woke up from his evening nap and COMPLAINED, "Oh, Darryl, your braying woke me up!"

How can you be concerned about sleeping, when I can't do what others can do?" Darryl cried.

Still sleepy and annoyed, Milo asked, "Now, what happened?"

"I can't walk long distances while carrying heavy loads on my back," Darryl said, "I am sure, my bones will break if I do."

"Can you do anything in your life?" asked Milo, **rolling** his eyes.

DARRYL IS UPSET

"You must have some **CONFIDENCE** in yourself, Darryl," said Flora the Flamingo, who was sitting nearby.

Flora was famous for her bright pink feathers, thin long legs and S-shaped neck. Flora gave two **lotuses** to Darryl and asked, "Do you think you can give one lotus to Milo?"

"Yes, I can," said Darryl, and gave one lotus to Milo.

"Hurray... Hurray... Finally, I heard Darryl say 'I Can'," clapped Flora. Both Milo and she laughed and congratulated

Darryl, who also smiled.

"Why are you not confident, Darryl?" asked Flora.

Making a sad face, Darryl replied, "Everyone makes jokes about donkeys as if we are of no use. Also, people often use the term 'donkey' or an 'ass' to insult others, to say they are slow or stupid."

Flora flapped her pretty wings and thought for a while.

"Come on, let's go for an evening stroll," she suggested, and the three of them started walking towards the LAKE.

EVERYONE HAS A STRENGTH

On the way, they met Ancy the Ant and her friends who were carrying food.

"Darryl, do you see the load on Ancy's back? Ants can carry weight that is 10 to 50 times their own body weight." Darryl watched Ancy and her friends, with AWE. "Such tiny creatures can do such a wonderful job!" he thought.

"*Croak... Croak...*" Suddenly Freddie the Frog came along. "I am practising for the long jump event in the next Annual Sports Meet," said Freddie.

"That's really amazing. Best wishes, Freddie," said Flora.

"A frog can jump almost 44 times its body length," explained Flora.

Though Darryl had seen frogs jump earlier, he noticed Freddie's jumping talent only today.

"Such a small creature can do such a wonderful job!" thought Darryl again. "But, they are talented by birth and I am born a fool," Darryl still believed.

"You must realise your strength and appreciate yourself," said Flora. "If you believe in NEGATIVE comments made by others, you will always doubt yourself and remain in fear."

Milo then explained, "Donkeys are strong and carry logs and grass. Do you know how they can really walk and carry the load long distances?"

"I know, yet nobody appreciates them. They are still called fools," Darryl replied glumly. "I simply cannot bear the pain of being called a fool. So I just walk around and eat and drink whatever I find."

LEARNING SOMETHING SPECIAL ABOUT ONESELF

"Do you know that donkeys are INCREDIBLE animals who have an excellent memory and tremendous physical strength? Believe that about yourself and work hard with a positive mind. Always say 'I Can'."

Darryl brayed suddenly, "Incredible animals!" he repeated.

"Studies have shown that donkeys can remember a place they have been to or recognise other donkeys who they met, even after 25 years. A donkey will not do something if it considers it to be unsafe. It can live more than 40 years and in various types of places," explained Flora.

Darryl was **STUNNED** to hear about the talents of his own kind.

Holding his large ear, Flora said, "Donkeys have large ears that help them **HEAR** across distances in deserts. If they sense something wrong while travelling, they will simply not move ahead and will dig in their heels."

CONFIDENCE BUILDS UP

"Am I really so strong and special?" asked Darryl. "I just can't believe it. I have heard something good about me for the first time."

Flora sat on Darryl's back and **PECKED** him gently, "Never compare yourself with others or try to copy them. Instead, find your own strengths and talents and believe in yourself. Always say 'I Can' so 'You Can."

Milo too jumped on Darryl's back and screamed, "Yes, we can!"

Darryl brayed, "Yes, I can..." and started running, jumping and dancing cheerfully with Flora and Milo on his back.

Darryl thanked Flora. He realised his own strengths and talents that made him smart, strong and confident!

A 'GHOST' STORY

By Ilika Priy

A young horse was very naughty so his parents named him Ghost.

One day, Ghost went deep into the FOREST looking for GRASS. Dumpy the Donkey saw him and said, "Hey, who are you? Are you new to the forest? I've never seen you here!"

"I am Ghost," said the horse.

A CHASE ENSUES

Dumpy heard that and GALLOPED away in fear. He did not want to be caught by a ghost!

Ghost did not understand why the donkey was running away and followed him. The two ran past Binoy the Bear. Dumpy shouted, "Binoy, run! There's a ghost behind me!"

"Ghost!" exclaimed Binoy. "There's no ghost behind you. That's a horse!"

"No, no. It's a ghost in the form of a horse!"

Just then, Ghost reached the two animals. Seeing him, Binoy and Dumpy **SCREAMED** and ran. Ghost ran after them. Seeing him following them, Binoy and Dumpy ran even faster. They saw Neo the Elephant on the way.

"Run, Neo! There's a ghost behind us!" shouted Binoy.

"There's a horse behind you!" said Neo.

"The horse is a ghost. Dumpy saw him turn from a ghost into a horse!" EXCLAIMED Binoy.

Neo also began running. He passed Buffy the Buffalo, and shouted, "Run, Buffy. There's a ghost chasing us in the form of a horse. He is saying he will eat us all. Run!"

Buffy was not sure whether to BELIEVE Neo. So she called out to Ghost, "Are you really a ghost?"

"Yes, I am Ghost," answered the horse.

Buffy began running after the other animals. "Run, run! A ghost is coming!"

All the other animals in the forest began running behind her.

Fatima the Fox saw the large group of animals running. "Why are you all running?" she asked.

"You may not believe in ghosts, but you will see one soon. If you don't run, it will eat you up!" shouted Binoy.

"A ghost! There's a ghost behind us!" the animals shouted.

Fatima burst out laughing. "You believe in ghosts? Is there anything like a ghost at all?"

"You may not believe in ghosts, but you will see one soon. If you don't run, it will eat you up!" shouted Binoy.

CLEARING UP MISCONCEPTIONS

"I'll wait to see it. What does a ghost look like? This looks like a horse!" saying that Fatima went close to Ghost. "Who are you?"

"I am Ghost," replied the horse.

"So, are you going to **eat** everyone here?"

"Why would I do that? I'm a horse. We eat grass!" exclaimed Ghost.

Fatima laughed again. "That's a funny ghost that only eats grass!" All the other animals stopped running and **STARED** at Fatima and Ghost.

"I'm a horse! My name is Ghost," explained Ghost.

Fatima laughed even harder.

"But didn't Dumpy see you change from a ghost to a horse?" asked Fatima.

"Oh no, I did not!" exclaimed Dumpy. "I asked who he was and he said he is a ghost. So I ran!"

"But Binoy told me you saw him change into a horse," said Neo.

Everyone turned to look at Binoy the Bear.

"I thought Dumpy saw him change into a horse. But I did not say he would eat us!" said Binoy, feeling uncomfortable.

"That was my guess," said Neo. Everyone laughed.

THE IMPORTANCE OF THINKING LOGICALLY

"Fatima, you were right to laugh. If you had not been here, we would still be running around with this rumour. Only after you stopped us did things become clear!" said Gigi the Goat.

"We need to think logically," said Fatima.

"Without logic, we will blindly TRUST everything we hear. If we think with a steady mind, we will find that some problems are in our imagination only."

"Fatima is right. We believed in the 'ghost' because we didn't want to understand the reality of the situation. Similarly, sometimes we just make an OPINION and stick to it. From now on, we should try not to believe in things without looking into the reason why something happened. Only then we will understand the real scenario before us," said Gigi. The other animals agreed.

"I am happy you all have realised that you should not blindly trust what you hear and see!" said Fatima.

The naughty Ghost was proud that he was responsible for spreading this awareness. Everyone left, promising to be more logical in the future.

SPOT THE DIFFERENCE

Circle 10 differences you can find between the two pictures.

LOOK BEFORE YOU LEAP

By Ramakant 'Kant'

There was once a jackal named Jared. When he was a cub and even before he could learn how to hunt properly, his parents were captured by poachers. He lived alone in the jungle and spent his time eating the remains off the kills of bigger animals.

One morning, when he felt particularly HUNGRY, he was having a tough time looking for food. He walked far and as he walked, he fell into a well. Fortunately, because of the hot summer months, the well had dried up and it wasn't too deep. Jared survived without a scratch.

But, the well was too deep for Jared to get out of on his own. He yelped and howled, asking for help but nobody came. He grew TIRED and sat down, with no idea of what was going to happen next. But suddenly, he heard footsteps. They were getting louder and louder with each step and they were approaching the well.

ONE BRIGHT IDEA!

When Jared looked up, there he saw the head of a goat. Jared knew that the goat was thirsty and was here in search of water.

Gigi the Goat had never felt this thirsty before. He had searched far and wide for water but had no luck so far. When he saw that the plants around the well were dry, a voice inside him told him that the well was probably dry. But he still decided to take a look and peeped in over the edge.

When he peeped, he did not see any water. All he saw was the shape of what looked like a tired jackal.

"Hey you down there," he said. "Is the WATER in there so sweet and so cool that you decided to jump in?"

Jared was so upset that he was going to be trapped in the well forever. But Gigi's words gave him hope.

"Why yes it is, my friend," he said. "When it gets too hot, I come here to cool off. The water is clear and a swim here makes my day."

Gigi was very thirsty and the idea of a well filled with cool water excited him. "All the watering holes around are dry yet this one isn't. But no one else is here. Doesn't anybody else know about this well?" he asked.

"If the other jackals knew this well existed, do you really think I'd be able to have so much fun?" asked Jared. "Come on in my friend, this well is big enough for both of us. JUMP in and enjoy the cool water that this well has to offer."

The idea of fresh, cool water was too tempting and Gigi jumped in.

FINALLY FREE!

Jared tried hard to hide his happiness. His plan was working perfectly. As soon as Gigi jumped into the well, Jared leapt with all his might onto Gigi's back and jumped out of the well.

Gigi was shocked. He couldn't understand what had happened. With his voice trembling, he asked, "My friend, why have you jumped out of the well and what happened to all the water that was here? Please, help me out of this well."

"Gigi, my friend, your stupidity has landed you into trouble. If you had spared even a moment to think of the consequences of your actions, you wouldn't have jumped into the well. Now it's time for me to go. I wish you good luck," said Jared and ran off.

Gigi was feeling sad. He sat at the bottom of the

well feeling helpless and soon fell asleep. He woke up when a pebble caught him hard on the top of his head. When he looked up, he saw Jared and with him were all the goats from Gigi's herd.

FRIENDSHIP

"I have come back for you my friend," said Jared. "If it wasn't for you, I'd be stuck in the well for the rest of my days. I wouldn't wish the same on you."

"Now do you understand why it's important to look before you leap, Gigi?" asked the other goats.

Jared and the goats pushed in big ROCKS and piles of dirt to make a platform inside the well. When it was high enough, Gigi jumped out of the well.

FORGETFUL PARI

By Prasanna Venkatesh

Pari the Squirrel, a school teacher was very forgetful. And this always got her into trouble.

THE CONSTANT MIX-UPS

Once when she was going to the market, she realized that everybody was **GIGGLING** at her. It was only after she checked her face in the store mirror, she knew why. Pari had forgotten to wash the soap off her face before leaving home.

Another time, the heater in her room was not

working. She called the electrician and said, "Please come immediately. I am in great trouble."

Within five minutes, she heard a SIREN and her door was broken down. Two men rushed in with a stretcher and tried loading her onto it. As it turned out, she had called the hospital instead of the electrician.

Needless to say, the paramedics were angry and Pari was embarrassed.

Yet another time, when she returned from school, she couldn't open her front door. She tried all the keys, but none of them worked.

When the lock was broken and she finally entered the house, she was shocked to find that the furniture looked different. Everything was placed elsewhere.

Later that evening somebody began ringing the bell furiously. When Pari opened the door, she understood why her keys didn't work. It wasn't her house.

While she lived on the 16th floor, Pari had mistakenly taken the elevator up to the 17th floor. The house owners were furious and Pari then spent a lot of money fixing the door.

Seeing how **scattered** her thoughts were, Pari's friend Kara the Cuckoo suggested that she make a list of all her day's **CHORES**.

While Pari made a list every morning, more often than not, she would forget where she left her list. She would waste time looking for it and this resulted in her being late.

PARI HAS TO GIVE A SPEECH

One morning, when Pari reached the school, the principal walked up to her and told her that she would be giving the Annual Day speech next week.

Pari was excited and determined to prove to others that she could be perfect for the job if she set her mind to it.

She prepared and finalised her speech the same day. In the evening she went to pick an outfit and found matching accessories. She spent all her free time rehearsing her every word.

Soon, from getting up from her seat to delivering the speech, to sitting back down, she knew it all.

A LONG WAIT IN THE AUDITORIUM

On the day of the function, she got ready before time and rehearsed again. Worried that she might board the wrong BUS, Pari took a taxi to school and kept checking her REFLECTION in the mirror. The last thing she wanted was for somebody to notice that she had applied lipstick on her eyes and kajal on her lips. Fortunately, she had made no such mistake.

She entered the school AUDITORIUM ahead of time and waited at her seat. She waited and waited but nobody arrived.

"Such indiscipline," she thought to herself. She waited some more and repeatedly checked her watch and still, there was no sign of anybody. At last, the peon, Prateek the Parrot entered the auditorium.

"Why are you so late?" she shouted at him. "Come on let's get the stage and the microphones ready. We are running late and I haven't rehearsed even once."

Prateek was utterly confused. "What are we getting the stage ready for?" he asked scratching his head.

"Don't tell me you've forgotten about the school's annual day function today," said Pari, still angry.

Prateek burst into laughter. "Ma'am, the function is tomorrow. Today is Sunday. Luckily I came in here to pick up my umbrella. Otherwise, you would have stayed here all day!"

Pari checked the date on the wall clock and realized he was right. She laughed at her own **folly** and went home.

Pari returned the next day and told this **anecdote** as part of her speech and got a big laugh from everyone present. They all **appreciated** her ability to laugh at herself.

WORDY JUMBLE

PUZZLE TIME

Match the words to complete them.

Pari has forgotten a few vowels in the words below.
Fill the missing vowels and guess the words.

O's, E's and A's are missing.

1. CHS ....
2. BND ....
3. DCD ....
4. QUL ....
5. FRT ....
6. PPR ....

* Answer on the last page

ANSWERS

PUZZLE TIME

Page 26: Treasure Find

Bobby the Bear and Justin the Bull will reach Goldie Gold island at 9:35AM. It will take 2 hours and 25 minutes to reach Isle Silvery Shiny. It will take 7 hours for them to reach the last port.

Page 52: Decode the Code

Santa is coming to town.

Page 64: Shadow Match

A - 8
B - 7
C - 2
D - 6
E - 3
F - 4
G - 5
H - 1

Page 95: Maze

Page 145: Wordy Jumble